CATNIP FOR THE SOUL

CATNIP FOR THE SOUL

Woody and Friends

AS TOLD TO JANE O'BOYLE

QUILL

WILLIAM MORROW

NEW YORK

It is the policy of William Morrow and Company, Inc., and its imprints and affiliates, recognizing the importance of preserving what has been written, to print the books we publish on acid-free paper, and we exert our best efforts to that end.

Library of Congress Cataloging-in-Publication Data

O'Boyle, Jane.
    Catnip for the soul / Woody and friends as told to Jane O'Boyle.
        p.   cm.
    ISBN 0-688-16982-1 (alk. paper)
    1. Cats—Humor.   2. Chicken soup for the soul—Parodies, imitations, etc.   I. Title.
PN6231.C23026   1999
814'.54—dc21   98–56004
                                                                CIP

Printed in the United States of America

First Quill Edition 1999

1   2   3   4   5   6   7   8   9   10

BOOK DESIGN BY JO ANNE METSCH

www.williammorrow.com

For
Joey Grimm,
Julie Grimm,
and Billy Grimm

with special thanks to
Michael Murphy,
Toni Sciarra,
and Charles Björklund

Contents

CATNIP FOR THE SOUL

Introduction

Being a cat is not easy. Ear mites. Hair and nail maintenance. Turf wars. Absent fathers. Chihuahuas.

And to top it off, no one ever writes books for cats about how to get rich and retire. No one goes on the lecture circuit to tell cats how to program their neurolinguistics and own real estate for nothing down. I've never seen a cat on *Oprah* or the *Today* show.

In compiling this book for fellow cats, I considered the value of putting forth strategies for selling more stuff and buying more stuff, but decided there was a greater need out there. This book is devoted to inspiring cats to higher levels of contentment and personal success. It's not about how to sell or buy more stuff. It's about how to get the stuff you cannot see for free.

Many of these stories are told in the voices of the cats who told me them in the first place. I'd like to thank them for their thoughtful and insightful contributions. Their pain was not easy to bring forward, as cats so rarely expose themselves in this way. I assured them that our readers would digest their tales most seriously. This book is dedicated to them.

Some stories here will make you sad; some will make

you happy. All of them will make you flick your tail and ponder the meaning of life.

Read this book slowly. Savor each morsel. If you want to share these stories with other cats, please do. Read them aloud to the cats who cannot read. Make these stories your own, so you can be inspired. Lick the wounds of your heart. Recharge your purr with a jumper cable. Wax your whiskers. You will, in turn, motivate others to do the same.

Reading this book will not only brighten your day and comfort your fellow cat, but it will also help inspire the humans around you. After all, people look to you for guidance — the important human Aldous Huxley (a writer during the Felix era) once advised his fellow people to observe cats "to mark, learn and inwardly digest the lessons about human nature which they teach."

Most of all, people look to you for love. But a cat must give love first to herself. The stories in this book are here to help you do that. Health, companionship, happiness, and love to all cats who wander on these pages.

— Woody

The Cat Bill of Rights

Pursuant to Article V of the U.S. Constitution

(A Public Service Reminder from the ACCLU)

ARTICLE I. Congress shall make no law prohibiting freedom of sleep, or the right of cats peaceably to assemble and to petition for a redress of grievances.

ARTICLE II. The right of cats to keep and bear claws shall not be infringed.

ARTICLE III. No cat shall in time of peace be quartered in any house, without the consent of the Owner's Cat, nor in time of war, but in a manner to be prescribed by law.

ARTICLE IV. ("The Friskies Act") The right of cats to be secure in their bodies, houses, papers, and effects, against unreasonable searches and seizures, shall not be violated.

ARTICLE V. No cat shall be held to answer for a capital, or otherwise infamous crime, unless on an indictment of a Grand Jury; nor shall any cat be subject for the same offense to be nine times put in jeopardy of life or limb; nor shall any cat be compelled in any criminal case to be a witness against herself.

ARTICLE VI. In all criminal prosecutions, the accused shall enjoy the right to a speedy and public catfight, and to have the assistance of a garden hose for his defense.

ARTICLE VII. The right of a trial by jury shall be preserved, except in cases where an electric can opener can be heard and the jury disperses, whereupon the accused shall be freed immediately.

ARTICLE VIII. Excessive bail shall not be required, nor cruel and unusual punishments inflicted, including the creation of little paper hats for photo opportunities.

ARTICLE IX. The enumeration of certain rights shall not be construed to deny or disparage others retained by the cats.

ARTICLE X. The powers not delegated to the United States by the Constitution, nor prohibited by it to the State, are reserved to the local cats respectively.

Throwing Up

Sometimes we have days or nights when our stomachs act up. I once heard a story about a young cat, Hector, who roamed his house from one room to another, coughing in agony when he should have been sleeping, searching for the right spot on the carpet to let it all out. He bumped into a human family member in the hallway, pacing restlessly like Hector even though it was the middle of the night and the person seemed not to have a hair ball or discernable ailment of any kind. He was simply unable to sleep for no good reason at all.

Hector coughed and dodged the hands of the human, not wanting to emit the fur ball in an awkward place. Finally, he spit the fur ball into a discreet corner of the hallway. Relieved and exhausted, he collapsed into happy slumber in an empty shoebox on the floor.

The person cleaned up after Hector and shook his head in amazement at the sleeping cat. Then, slowly, the person became aware of the simple restful lesson of a nocturnal feline event. Staying awake for anything

other than a violent stomachache or hair ball elimination was not a reason to stay awake at all. And so the
human went to bed and fell asleep, just like Hector in
the box.

—Kitty from Ypsilanti

Flying

Taking an airplane ride is never enjoyable. However, it is more tense for the humans on board than it is for you. You can at least distract yourself by studying the shoes and feet of the people around you. You can imitate the engine sounds by making siren noises, which will entertain the crowd. The people will smile at you, even though they are more nervous and afraid than you are. Some will frown at you, but they are the most frightened of all, and you can always frown back at them if you want to. They know, should the plane experience an unscheduled landing, that you will be the first one to reach the emergency exit, no matter what row you're sitting in. But that rarely happens. The important thing to remember about flying is this: It is the only time in your life you will soar higher than every bird on earth.

— *Woody*

Spell It Out

Not long ago, I conducted an informal experiment. The power of suggestion is so prevalent in the human species that my goal was to see if it also exists in cats. I got a few of my friends together in the Powells' barn. While listening to Sammy sing a song, I leaned over and started cleaning my behind. I watched covertly to see if others would do the same. Sure enough, one by one, my friends started to lean over in various ways to do some private grooming of their own. Even Sammy gave a sigh and pushed himself over toward his rear end.

But then I noticed an even more unusual phenomenon. I suppose all great discoveries take place by happenstance. Anyway, I was struck by how Zuzu's hind legs formed a large letter "K" in the air while she leaned over to clean her bottom. Puff turned herself into a giant "L," and Clem's legs formed a "C," but his tail sticking up made him look more like an "E." One-eyed Bob had started cleaning his armpit instead, but this made his arm stick out like another "E." Fluff had her giant feet in the air while her nose was below, propped up by one forearm, which turned her into an

"N." The kitties were spelling "kleen"! I went wild with my discovery and ran around bouncing off the barn walls. The cats paused to look at me, blinked, then resumed their activity. I finally stopped, out of breath, to watch them cleaning themselves in oblivious synchronicity.

Everything we do makes sense because we spell it out for you! Cats are really quite simple to understand, if you only pay attention.

—Mr. Reilly

Turf

Like all cats, I do my best to keep strangers out of my yard. It's not that I'm unfriendly, it's just a cat thing (*cosa gatto*, if you will) to maintain neighborhood diplomacy. I can't keep squirrels out, or dogs, or people, so I might as well do all I can to keep out other cats—or at least make it clear who's the chief honcho of this yard. I respect other cats who do the same.

However, in a manic mouse chase I might inadvertantly enter the domain of my neighbor. If you're fielding a home run, do you stop running just because a wall is there? My point exactly. All I want to do is make the catch. Please respect my need to win the game. I'll get outta your yard as soon as I've got the little guy between my teeth.

—Mario

Driving

Some cats like riding in cars and some don't. Those who do can sit in whatever seat they choose, except the driver's seat. Those who don't, like Punky, learn how to sit in their carriers and meditate, waking drowsily when the window gets rolled down and new smells waft in. If the smells emanate from a tollbooth, she yawns and puts herself back into the zone. Too many fumes. If the smells indicate her final destination, she cranes her neck to ensure it is not the vet's office. If it is the vet's office, she hisses like the bride of Frankenstein. If it's any other place, she simply moans politely.

We struggle with cars because we know that they are not our friends—cars have taken the lives of so many cats we know. But the best relationship to have with a car is to be inside it. After all, if you are inside the car, it cannot run over you. You are more safe inside the car than outside. Thank the fates for putting you there. And watch the trees go by.

—Colonel Purrker

Angel Fleas

Some kitties look at fleas as being bothersome. Others, like old Pepper, have learned that fleas can bring blessings in itchy disguise.

Pepper was feeling down. Two of her neighborhood friends had succumbed to leukemia, and an old street injury was aggravating her tendinitis. When fleas moved in under her tail and behind her left ear, she felt she might as well hang up her ice skates and retire. It seemed nothing was going right for her. Achingly, she began the ritual of scraping the fleas from her neck with her toenails. After a while, she was begrudgingly dunked into a warm bath. By then she didn't even have the energy to scrape her paws down the sides of the bathtub to try to stop the immersion.

But you know what happened? The leg exercise of scratching the fleas, plus the warm baths, relieved her tendinitis after years of suffering. As a result of the "pet's curse," Pepper was cured. Sometimes a difficult period can bring you new appreciation of how wonderful life can be.

— Woody

Trees

I cannot climb a tree. There: I said it. I was raised in the city and, even though I'm an adult now and live in the country, I never took climbing lessons or got my license. Oh sure, I have all my claws. I simply choose not to damage them in that endeavor.

Some cats think I'm missing out on something, not climbing trees. But it's not true. I learn some of life's most important lessons from trees. I look at them. I watch the birds and squirrels up there. I use the trunks as scratching posts. I relate to a tree on a different level. I use it for a higher purpose, like pondering life's mysteries. I feel bad that the tree never gets to leave the yard and is stripped of its cover when the weather turns cold. I wouldn't like that very much.

Who cares about climbing trees? All we do is get stuck in them anyway. And I don't know about your town, but where I live, they don't have firefighters who rescue cats in trees anymore. My next-door neighbor Titus tried that attention-getting ruse last summer. As expected, he got a lot of attention from hand-wringing women and children. But the emergency trucks would not respond. No sirens. No ladders. Nothing. What

Titus thought would be a show-stopper of an afternoon turned into a humiliating solo descent, on his own four legs, to a disappointed crowd who realized Titus hadn't been in any danger after all.

If I could climb a tree, shoot, I'd get just as carried away with my self-importance as old Titus did. I think I'm better off keeping all four feet on the ground. Who wants to look down? I'd much rather look up.

—Geronimo

Eating Etti-kit

Enjoying your meals is the sign of good health. Most of us have no problem with that. However, it still confounds this cat that people think we prefer to eat on the floor. They sit with decorum at the table, at a proper height over their food, with colorful placemats to catch the crumbs, and with their food served on pretty dishes painted with fish or bird designs. We would enjoy those things, too. A little table would be nice, so we wouldn't have to practically lie down for a quick munch. Would an old cast-off box be a big expense? Pretty ceramic dishes instead of dingy rubber ones. A placemat to catch what our little tongues inadvertantly lap off. Can't they see that when we drop food by accident, we don't eat the splashes off the floor? They remain on the floor, a dry and crusty reminder that our table service could use some adjustment.

I try leaping on the big table to give them a hint, but they still don't get it. I try to peer into their fancy china so they can see how much I admire the dishes. I'll keep trying. But don't worry: I won't miss a meal in the meantime.

—*Silver*

Vinnie's Nine Niftiest
Places for a Morning Nap Rotation

1. Southwest corner of big bed
2. Bathroom rug
3. Laundry basket (if full)
4. Northwest corner of big bed
5. The kid's empty backpack
6. Pile of mittens in back hall closet
7. East end of living room sofa
8. Large ceramic bowl on coffee table (summer only)
9. Heating vent near guest room closet

Licking

We take comfort in the small, repetitive actions that comprise our day. We love to be clean, too. But it's more than that. When we bathe ourselves, we're recalling the comforting moments when Mom did this for us in her soothing way, showing her love. We can never get enough of it. Do it for another cat from time to time — a friend, a coworker, a distant relative — and feel the purring appreciation for giving someone else that love, too. If you enjoy licking, you'll keep on ticking.

—Frodo

No Tail, but Many Tales

Some cats complain about discrimination from humans for being associated with witches and bad luck. When you're a cat, you either please people like punch or you scare their pants off. When you're a cat who has no tail, the popularity meter moves to even greater extremes. When you're a cat with no tail, cat-loving people love you even more than they do all other cats. They know you stand apart from the rest. You are Manx, from the Isle of Man, and this is an important place for creatures who call themselves man.

On the other hand, people who don't like cats think a tailless cat is a stomach-turning voodoo curse, a walking testament to why all cats are freaks of nature, as if all humans are perfectly formed. These people see me, and the hair stands up on the backs of their necks. (Did you ever notice how a cat-hating person acts like a cat—cautious, tense, secretive, and stubborn?) This reaction used to get me down, but now I'm used to it. After all, they don't have a tail, either! I'm more like they are than they even know.

— Gumby

Claws

I don't spend a lot of time at the manicurist. I like to care for my own nails. When I'm alone, I stretch my arm out and extend my digits so I can admire them. These claws are so cool. They are perfect. They tap-tap-tap on bare floors, like delicate high heels. They sink into trees, carpets, and chipmunks like a hot knife through butter. And they almost never break. I sometimes wish I could paint them, like people do. But the best part about my claws is that, as terrific as they are, they are modestly concealed beneath my toes most of the time. One moment I'm Puss-in-Boots but, in a jam, I'm Freddie Krueger. I like that. For, as everyone knows, your greatest power is the part of you no one can see.

— *Coquette*

On Crossing the Street

We can't help it. We hear the car approaching and we know it will be a dangerous encounter, but we can't ignore our instincts. We have enough common sense to pause and think about it. We prick up our ears and sweep them around 90 degrees in case we might hear something happening elsewhere to distract us. But all we hear is the chipmunk foraging under the dead leaves on the other side of the road. The rubber tires are getting closer, but the rustling is getting louder in our ears. With every second, as the car approaches, the chipmunk's crunching becomes more impossible to resist. Finally, we dash into the street, right under the deadly wheels. Some of us make it. Some of us surrender the last life we have.

What makes us so impulsive? Why don't we just tip our ears to the chipmunk, so happy in his endeavors across the road? He is not in our way; he's just minding his own business, providing for his family. Instead of desiring to impale and shred him, what would happen if we lifted our whiskers and smiled at the chipmunk? The chipmunk would have a better day, and we would all live to tell about it tomorrow.

— *Woody*

On Curling Up into a Ball

In a box,
in a bag,
in a basket,
on a rag:
Any of them
brings thoughts of you
and how you held me
all night through.
Thanks, Mom.

—Gordon

O Christmas Tree

When trees suddenly appear inside your house, they usually have very odd fruits and flowers growing on them. These are mysterious plants you almost never see in the wild, and it is your job to investigate and identify them. Fortunately, this is not an arduous assignment, as these trees are covered with bright, shiny, crinkly or crackly, bouncy, and riveting objects of pure cat joy.

The trees themselves are usually a climbing challenge, for people seem to think thicker is better when it comes to indoor foliage. Also, the roots have been amputated so the tree cannot maintain its usual balance for your liberal exploration. In other words, if you weigh more than eight pounds, you will knock the tree over. For some, this is part of the challenge.

One cat I know uses the blanket-covered base as a festive Johnny-on-the-spot. He thinks he's outdoors, apparently. This cat shall remain nameless.

Christmas trees have a short life span, so do your work quickly. Avoid biting on the camouflaged electrical wires. If you can't scale the tree at all, then at least kill the low-hanging fruit along the bottom. You can usually then pull down the tree to get at the rest. *Joyeux Noel!*

—Jules

Hair

We like to show off our fur coats. No other domestic creature has such a natural, soft pelt that everyone wants to touch. It is our pride. And each coat is completely different. It sets us apart, attracts admirers, keeps us warm and cool, soft and fuzzy. I once saw a cat with no hair and, I have to tell you, he didn't look like a cat at all. I can't imagine that guy has any of the same feline experiences I do. He looked kind of like a rat. In fact, I kind of wanted to eat him. Now, how strange is that? It's not his fault, I know. I never realized that aside from its natural beauty, fur covers up a war zone of warts, wrinkles, scars, and birthmarks. No one needs to see such imperfections, no matter how slight. Even in oneself. Today I am even more thankful that God blessed me with this coat.

— Woody

Some Cat Rules

1. You will remain lithe and beautiful all your life.

2. Receiving one meal does not mean you will always get another. Keep track of your bowl. If it is not refilled, start looking for alternative things to eat.

3. Your people are mirrors of you. They reflect the things about yourself you either love or hate.

4. Never date a cat the same day you meet him. The cats who do this always get into trouble.

5. Journal: Record your daily impressions by scratching the back of the sofa every day.

—Bullet

Snoozing

Don't ever get caught short of sleep. When we dream, we recall our collective unconscious of night-prowling in the forest, stalking the prey of our ancestors, and bonding with our pride. Sleeping is what separates cats from nearly every other creature. It is who we are. Some might tease us about our proclivity for napping, but they are the ones who do not sleep enough. Sleeping makes us serene and fulfilled and enables us to be fully, instantly awake when the need arises. In fact, lie down on this book right now and take a quick siesta. You've been awake too long. Sweet dreams, *querida*.

— *Carlos*

Lady Cat

For some reason, I have never had kittens. Just the same, I was born with the instinct to feed others and to teach them how to kill. I do have two large adult humans who appear to be quite helpless in this area. So, I am raising them as though they were my own kittens.

To begin with, I bring them a fresh kill from the yard every morning. A warm shrew, a fat mouse, a vole omelet. When my people come to the door to let me in, I sit next to my kill and tell them that this is very nourishing food and that they really should give it a try. They respond, as most juveniles do, with a groan or a squeal of distaste. I pick it up to bring it in the house, and they shout "No!" and slam the door in my face. I don't think real kittens are quite this difficult. I look down at my fresh kill and sigh. Across the street, the invisible fence is zapping Brandy the Irish setter. Who can explain the mysteries of life?

The front door opens and my human number one picks me up and carries me to a large bowl of warm imitation-mouse meat loaf. She pets me behind the ears as she puts me down. You don't always have to be the one who takes care of everybody. Sometimes it's time to let someone else take care of you.

—Misty

When Fighting Is Good for You

Some believe we should always try to keep the peace. I disagree. Arguing with another cat can really get your juices flowing and remind you that the free world is filled with an amazing variety of opinions. The best fight I ever had was in the heating duct of a house that was being renovated. I encountered a burgler cat in the vent, and we promptly had a set-to, in stereo, that woke the whole family. Everyone joined in the fun, shouting and running and letting every emotion run forth. I dashed around the heat ducts, chasing my adversary, laughing with the joy of slinky movement. Go ahead, make your day. Pick a good fight with one of your neighbors, release some energy, shake up some hormones, and bring everyone together for a rollicking good time.

— Gimbel

The Dogs I Love

There are six: Abbie, Harper, Franki, Willie, Zoe, and Big Boy. Dogs I sort of like, but wish weren't so rambunctious: Hugo and Hannibal. Dogs I don't like at all: Millie, Casey, and Prince. Dogs I used to like, but they went away: Barney, Trevor, and Jake.

I cannot fathom why some dogs are the size of cats, yet they don't behave like cats. When I am around a small dog, I become a little removed because I don't want anyone to mistake me for a small dog, too. I might actually look away and pretend I am not acquainted with the little dog at all, lest I be in any way associated with jittery nutcase behavior.

I have slowly come to accept the dog elements of my own nature. I know it isn't easy for a cat to do; harder even than a dog trying to accept his cat side. But a real cat admits to his canine tendencies and embraces them. The dog I love the most, I suppose, is the one hidden deep within myself.

— Woody

People's Children

They may be bratty, whiny, and stinky, they may pull your tail and dress you in crazy outfits, but people's children are always fun. They are needy: They always want you to stay even when you want to go. But the truth is, we always want them to stay, too. I like to think of them as oversize mice. Bat them around for a while, torture them right back, and we all have a great time. And they are impossible to destroy. As they grow old, they are less fun, but then so are we.

You won't stand for wearing a doll dress when you're old and cranky. Cherish the passions of youth while they are yours.

—Sadie

Neuteronomy

Cat family planning is a personal thing. But people usually assume that you intend to enter into intimate relations with others and they can't always tell from the outside if you are using birth control, so sometimes they help you make the decision. If you don't have a life filled with erotic encounters, don't feel bad. There are tons of sexually transmitted diseases out there, which can turn a cat's life into a dog's life. And, without sex, there is that much more time to snack, take naps, and catch up on gossip at the scratching post.

—Clem

Vinnie's Nine
Niftiest Snacks

1. Salmon croquettes
2. Mouse
3. Catnip
4. Lay's potato chips
5. Carrot shavings (must be fresh)
6. Bran flakes (watch portions!)
7. Bird
8. Tulip stems (not heads)
9. Water from birdbath*

*Note: Moths nearly tied for ninth place.

Blue Bloods

Watching TV, commuting, shopping, hunting, one is constantly exposed to sophisticated advertising. A cat sometimes finds it difficult to maintain high self-esteem. Not everyone can be a Paulina Persian or a Princess Burmese. Very few cats Concorde it to France or live at the Plaza. But if we work together in our very own homes to boost our cat image among our loved ones, we can make more of a difference than any ad campaign.

Plus-sized Puss or Harried Housecat, make this your motto: Yes, I can do anything! Then try it. Leap from the mantel to the piano. Grab that five-pound ham off the table. Open that locked door. You can have twenty-four toes, one eye, half an ear, and no tail, but you can still win the contest of style and panache. If you have the right attitude, you will be surprised at what you can achieve.

— Trixie

If I Had My Nine Lives
to Live Over

I would eat more striped bass.

I would make friends with more humans.

I would give back life to the bat I killed—I didn't
know what it was until it was too late.

I would establish USDA regulations for cat food
manufacturers.

I would say "I love you" more often.

I would pick more catnip.

—Marble, age 23

The Cats on Mars

We saw them on the *Pathfinder* photos, though most people did not. They were there. I saw an ear poking out from behind a red rock. Fuzzy saw the shadow of one stalking along underneath the vehicle as it moved. Gunnar saw familiar scratch marks in the red sand. We discussed among ourselves the cats who live up there without water or milk. People did not notice these things because they are oblivious to familiar creatures other than their bipedal selves. Unlike humans, we cats already speak a universal language. That makes us earthlings of a higher order than humans, because cats long ago engineered a single common language. Therefore, understanding messages from another planet is no effort at all. We know the Martian cats were somewhat fearful of being invaded and colonized by humans. But then the vehicle broke down and, not surprisingly, the people's interest in Mars faded away. That's one small step for mankind, and one giant leap for felines on the planet where cats still reign.

— Gumball

Sleeping with Humans

I like to nap on Mom and Dad's bed. The kids' beds are not large enough for me. The other reason I prefer my parents' bed is because, well, because Mom and Dad don't really want me there. They take up an awful lot of room, a lot more than I do. They push me off in their sleepy state, they kick me, they tell me to go sleep with the kids. But I don't mind. I try to sleep in between them, until Dad wakes up and shoves me away. Then I lumber over to the edge on Mom's side. She ends up moving closer to Dad. I like to see them closer together. Dad wakes up first and leaves, then I sprawl out all over his side. When Mom gets up, she tries to pull the blanket over my head. Sometimes I jump to the floor and watch her make the bed, then I jump back up and snooze on the covers. And wait for them to return.

—Kitty from New York

The Cat's Meow

Most of us don't say much because we already know that we know everything. And efficient communication is a feline trademark. But Boots meows nonstop. He's a little unsure of himself, I suppose, so he expresses his opinion about everything. Whenever anyone walks into the room, he starts yapping. For all I know, he's still yapping after everybody leaves. He just likes to hear himself talk. He meows about dogs he saw out the window, about dreams he had last night, about what kind of food he wants for dinner, about where he plans to take his next nap. He's still talking about the day his people left him alone in the dark for two days.

He talks to cats, to dogs, to people. He veritably wastes his words. He meows so much, most of us ignore him now. Just like we turn our backs on the gabby human. They are the ones who do not listen. Why should we listen to them?

—Kahlil

Callie's Top Ten List of Warmest Spots in the House

1. Top of stove, over pilot light
2. Cable box on top of TV
3. Desktop, under lamp
4. Any human head
5. Heat vent under bathroom sink
6. Shifting sunbeam in foyer
7. Clothes dryer
8. Computer hard drive
9. Box of sweaters under small bed
10. Windowsill in powder room (mornings)

Dreams

I watch an eland on the vast plain with a breeze blowing through the tall grass. That's where I'm hiding. The animal is grazing in a field, turning his back to me—a foolish piece of meat who should fear me more than he obviously does. He may not be smart, but I know he's fast.

I have much patience and I enjoy waiting for him as he grazes closer to me. The breeze halts, the grass stands straight, and the animal's head bolts upward. I make a victorious leap.

I don't know where this dream comes from, since I've never seen such an animal in real life and I've never been to such a plain. Could it be true what they say about the collective unconscious of cats? Or am I really a Siberian tiger, only at night? If I see a deer in my backyard today, what should I do about it? Next time I'm at the vet, I'll bring up these questions. Someone has to know the answers.

—Macy

Nine Lives

Some people think the trouble with having nine lives is that we tend to take each life for granted. We live boldly, climbing too high, jumping into dangerous holes, leaping from one rooftop to another, attacking muskrats who are larger than we are. We live so daringly, it's true, that sometimes we lose count of which life we're on. But I don't see the point in treating even the ninth life delicately. What fun is it to stop chasing squirrels, stop leaping fences, and stay away from warm car engines? Humans have only one life, but that doesn't stop them from doing silly things.

Don't stop reaching for the very best life has to offer. Live every life not as if it were your last; live it as if it were your first.

— Sammy

My Favorite Menu

For my dinner, it must be meat. As a cat and a protein lover, I don't need to eat a single fruit or vegetable in my entire life. I am very pleased by this.

The exact selection of meat is immaterial to me. Freshness is important. Fins are fun to crunch on, but then so are wings. I prefer my meat very rare, but cooking doesn't ruin it completely.

Canned food is just fine, too. Especially when it's been microwaved for ten seconds. This warms chilled food to fresh mouse temperature. And the gravy is terrific!

However, there is one type of food people rarely offer me, and it's one of my favorites: dessert. Ice cream, bread pudding, creme caramel, baked Alaska, cannoli, profiteroles, tiramisu, cheesecake. I shouldn't have it all the time, but dessert is good for me. It's motor oil for my purr engines.

When it's time for dessert, please don't forget the sweetest member of your family. Me.

—*Rocky*

The Generals Among Us

Some cats have a single-colored coat. Some cats have patches of color. Some look like they're wearing cardigan sweaters, with their white chests and feet showing.

Whatever our color, we are all created equal. There is no discrimination based on color in the cat world. Never has been. But it is rarer and rarer to find the cat with stripes.

People think stripes are just a matter of the gene pool lottery. Lucky stripes. But cats know stripes have to be earned. Wisdom and experience are reflected in stripes. Some kittens may be born with stripes, but most will lose them as they grow older, just as a human baby loses hair.

The cats with guts will gain stripes as they age. The cats who serve valiantly in battle with integrity, honesty, valor. The ones who provide a role model for the feline race. Some have stripes you can see only in morning sunlight, because they modestly asked that their stripes be the same color as their natural coats.

We respect the striped among us. When we pass a

striped cat on the street, we salute him with a flick of our tails. We step aside and respectfully lower our ears to him. Teach your kitties well, and maybe they'll grow up to have stripes, too.

— Beau

Crowning Glory

Stripes must be earned, but hair length is simply a matter of genetic chance. I have short hair and I turn a little green when I see another cat with beautiful long tresses. But I remind myself how much extra cleaning such beauty demands. And the discomfort of humid summers when long hair turns into clumps and mats. Not to mention the frequent digestive obstructions (if my hair balls are bad now, imagine having two or three times as much hair!).

My natural crew cut is cleaned with a simple shake of the booty. It may appear I got the short end of the stick. When I was a kit, I used to think so. But now, shucks, I am thankful every day that I have hair at all.

— Woody

Positions

When I take a nap, I often stretch all my paws into the air and let my tummy catch some rays. Not many cats are so trusting of the outside world, and some call me foolish. Maybe a wild animal will make a play for my gut. Other cats ask me where I learned to do this. I suppose I learned it from my human family. They look so happy, stretched out in the hammock or lounging on the sofa. Oh, I still curl up into a ball most of the time. But if you want to add variety to your sleeping life, try doing it like a person, on your back.

—Nico

What's Wrong with TV Today

There aren't enough cats on TV shows. There are plenty of dogs on TV, that's for sure. And there are kids' shows that star fake cats, like Tom and Jerry, Ren and Stimpy, and Garfield. Not a single show with a real cat. Some animals even become the star, like Lassie, Mr. Ed, Arnold the pig, Kermit the frog—none of whom achieved the feats of any ordinary cat.

Seinfeld may not have been a cat person, but Drew Carey has to be. I think having a cat would make Ally McBeal a happier person. Frasier is obviously a cat lover, but there's a big blank in his apartment where the pet cat should be. And the friends on *Friends* are missing one big fat purring animal. How real is that? Dan Rather would loosen up more if he tried a cat on the set. Oprah won't make me cry until she does a whole show devoted to Cat Rescues. Some say Jerry Springer's show has catfights, of all things, but I have yet to see one.

This is what's really wrong with TV today. Without a cat, the shows just don't seem real. Sure, they have news, advice, laughs. But they have no soul.

— Owl

Working Cats and Stay-at-Home Cats

All cats work for a living. We treat each other as equals because none of us has it easier than any other. Me, I am a mouser in a small grocery store. I get an awful lot of benefits, not even including the mice I catch. I get scraps of sardines and mortadella from the deli counter, rub-downs from the people who visit the store, and there's a great garbage can out back, when I can get to it. I wouldn't stay home if you paid me.

Hershey, he's a house cat. He stays indoors all day, sitting on window sills, drinking milk from saucers. He gets a little stressed out because there's no one to play with and no mice to catch. He says he's happy, though, and I have no reason to doubt him. It's not a matter of money or chance. It's a matter of the heart. I wouldn't trade places with Hershey for the world. But God love him if he thinks his life is what being a cat is all about.

—Daisy

Listen to Your Whiskers

I live in the South. Magnolia trees, crabs, hot tin roofs. And it's very convenient because there's never any snow to block access to mouse holes. There are lots of great rivers and ponds and swamps down here, where birds and fish hang out. But as a rule, we stay away from these watering holes, tempting though they may be. Our whiskers tell us: The 'gator lives in these waters. To the alligator, we are a walking hot meal to go. I hate to think of all the fun things I'm missing down at the pond, but I know better than to ignore what the whiskers tell me.

Some humans have whiskers, though they are not as handsome as mine. But people never listen to their whiskers. Most people even cut them off on a daily basis, so irritated are they by what the whiskers say. And then they wonder why they have only one life, while we have nine. Some people never learn.

— Woody

Red Robin Blues

(for slide guitar)

Robin sings the blues
Flown a mile in those shoes
Missed the worm
Tipped the booze
Chirps all day
Not amused
Burning both ends of the fuse
This cat's got to break the news
He's got one more thing to lose
He's a meal I sure could use
Robin, don't you sing the blues
No more.

—*Muddy*

Vinnie's Nine Niftiest Hobbies

1. Batting around cloth mice
2. Opening kitchen cupboards and checking pots and pans for future nap reference
3. Flipping over a corner of the welcome mat and scratching a while
4. Locating new spots of sunshine on the carpet
5. Listening for mice in the walls and seeking out new ways to get in there with them
6. Testing human laps for comfort
7. Walking along the back of the sofa
8. Flirting with Chloe next door
9. Snoozing

Forbidden Fruit

For all the flying creatures we love to stalk and catch, there is one we always leave alone: the butterfly. The fact that he doesn't have much meat on him is only part of the reason we don't prey on this floating picture. It's also his wings. The wings are a signal to a cat: They say "we are magic fairies of peace. Do not eat us." It fascinates me to watch the butterfly. Mostly, I am in awe of the fact that I do not want to eat him. After all, I love a good juicy moth as much as the next cat. Isn't a butterfly just a moth with tattoos? The answer, my friend, is no. This illustrated butterfly, he is an angel. Do your best to protect and admire, but never, never touch.

Also in the forbidden category: salamanders and turtles. The salamander is most satisfying to chase, but impossible to catch, as he disappears like a ghost. He is considered good luck by all creatures, including people. A cat who catches the salamander will be cursed for all his lives.

The turtle, he is slow and clumsy. This is no challenge to a mighty cat like me. He may be tasty, but he is too easy. The turtle is the lazy cat's kill. Or rather, the foolish cat's kill, for those who try it often have a

limb snapped off by the jaws of the wily turtle. You will
be branded lazy for a lifetime, if you survive at all.

So many wonderful things to eat in your backyard.
But remember, *mio gatto*:

> Butterfly, never try;
> Salamander, curse your dander;
> Turtle meat, not so sweet.

> — *Pablo*

Scratching Posts

My mom spent $47 for a carpeted post with a curved bench seat on top. It has my name on it. It's very stimulating. It has coarse rope wound around the pedestal, and I can dig my claws in any hour of the day or night. The bucket seat is just large enough for me to curl up in. Or I can let my arms and legs dangle over the side. I can let my head hang over, too. I love this scratching post. I use it every chance I get.

But there's an even bigger scratching post in the living room. It cost $1,269. It's got two big cloth posts on either end and a huge bench seat where I can sprawl all over the place. Okay, so it's the couch. And Mom hates it when I scratch it. But if I didn't scratch it, she wouldn't pay so much attention to me. So I get in a little mischief now and then, simply to know I'm loved.

—Emmers

Cookies

Nothing beats a mouse or a fish, but there are certain "vegetarian" people treats that I find tasty. A Fig Newton is divine. Could it be that this cookie is really made from minced mice? It looks like a pig-in-a-blanket. Maybe it's really a guinea-pig-in-a-blanket. I cannot believe whatever is ground up in there is not meat of some kind. Why else do I crave it so?

People tell me I have a sweet tooth. No, it is a meat tooth. I know. But let them believe what they will. It's their treat, after all. Let us not tell the humans what's really in a Pig Newton. I mean, a Fig Newton.

—Jumper

Nesting Tips

A shoebox is very nice to curl up in. But if you're jumbo sized like I am, a boot box is twice as nice. Paper bags from the grocery store are fun because they make noise when you get inside. Christmas boxes frequently contain crinkly tissue paper, which provides loads of noisy entertainment before you settle down to sleep. Baskets are quiet, but the straw is very soothing to scratch on before you get comfy.

Yin and Yang often share a round basket, forming a swirled two-toned perfect circle. Yin claims Yang takes up more than half the space, which is true. Personally, I am happy not to have to share my basket with anyone!

The cardboard cartons that computer paper comes in have high walls for protection from curious siblings.

The important thing to remember about a container is how well it holds you. If it feels like a hug, then make yourself snug.

— *Woody*

The Green-Eyed Monster

Some say I am jealous of the new baby, the old dog, the mother-in-law, and the gray van in the driveway. Well, these things do get the attention that rightly belongs to me. And yet, Mrs. Rodgers next door feeds me chopped liver with whipped cream. I think she loves me even more than my own parents do. And she even has three cats of her own already.

It's tempting to move in permanently with Mrs. Rodgers, and she tries awfully hard to entice me. This occupies my thoughts during the day. But recently, I was heading home on the sidewalk when I saw my mom, my old dog, and my new baby out for a walk. They smiled and asked me to join in. I felt proud. For at Mrs. Rodgers' house, I'm cat number four. In my crowded family, I'm cat number one.

—Mittens

In a Cat's Eye

Polly met Chester in the vestibule at the vet's office. Chester's mom told Polly's mom that Chester was missing a leg because he'd been hit by a car. Polly studied Chester closely. She couldn't see anything missing. He was friendly and loving. He was even cute, with his ears cast aside at a rakish angle. He was 100% cat. Polly realized that humans look on the outside to judge another. Cats look at one another and see only the inside. If Chester were unloved or bitter, well, Polly would have seen that. To her eyes, Chester had all four legs, as strong and fast as a cheetah's. Chester looked at Polly, shrugged his shoulders, and winked.

—Leo

The Vacuum Cleaner

As you know, there are many things that fascinate cats for no apparent reason. Some kitties I know are afraid of vacuum cleaners, but I find them enthralling. They don't all look the same or sound the same. Mine is called Hoover, but other breeds are called Electrolux, Eureka, and Dirt Devil. Big or small, loud or humming, they have enormous appeal to me. And I have never once been sucked up a vacuum's giant nostril, try though it might to get me. I am very clever.

Someone once told me the vacuum is descended from an ancient creature who, in the wild, would make a tempestuous rout through the forest with every quarter moon. Seemingly out of nowhere, it would roar over the mossy woods carpet, claiming any animal in its path. These creatures became extinct, however, and modern vacuum cleaners are all man-made now. I suppose we should be thankful they're still around at all, to keep a cat alert and swift.

—Princess

Cosa Nostra

There are mice in this world who go about demanding to be killed. You must have noticed them. They quarrel in gambling games, they jump out of their holes in a rage if someone so much as scratches the wall, they humiliate and bully creatures whose capabilities they do not know. I have seen such a mouse, a fool, deliberately infuriate a group of dangerous cats, and he himself without any resources.

These are mice who wander through the world shouting, "Kill me, kill me." And there is always someone ready to oblige them. We see it every day. These mice of course do a great deal of harm to others also.

Since such a mouse does not fear death and indeed looks for it, the trick is to make yourself the only cat in the world who he truly desires *not* to kill him. He has only one fear, not of death, but that *you* may be the one to kill him. He is yours then.

— Clemenza

I Love a Parade

Computers and videos are taking the place of three-dimensional pageants, sacred rituals, and old-fashioned, warm-blooded hijinx and hilarity. "Live action" means just the opposite, it seems. So every once in a while, I like to get the gang together for a parade. As you know, most people don't want to watch a parade — they want to march in the parade!

So we promenade down Main Street with the whole works. Sammy is in the marching band, banging the drum with his fat tail. Boots rides on the Purina float of catnip blossoms. Sweetie Pie leads five other cats, each one holding a string by her tail for the giant Garfield balloon. The Gallagher quadruplets are harnessed to a buggy and pull Elliott, dressed in a pelican costume. Everyone can tell it's Elliott because his crumpled ear is showing. It is a joyful ritual, celebrating the pleasure of just being a cat.

Next year, I'm planning a new theme in honor of Bastet, the Egyptian cat goddess. Our floats are going to be little pyramids and moving sphinxes, with four hairy legs apiece. If you see us coming down your street, please slow down and move to the side. Thank you.

—*Puddinhead*

The Ironies of Nature

Cats know everything, including the fact that we are no longer king of the forest. To prove the point to kittens, I frequently enumerate the number of birds who are larger than we are. There are also a number of tasty fish who are bigger than a cat. Many of these animals have human laws and even cat laws protecting them. Therefore, we must treat these birds and fish with respect. Do not try to kill one of these by yourself.

Heron	Shark
Pelican	Marlin
Goose	Tuna
Swan	Dolphin
Peacock	Squid
Turkey	Salmon
Condor	Barracuda
Eagle	Mackerel

Vulture   Grouper

Ostrich   Flamingo

Pheasant   Parrot

Crane   Owl

—Waldo Lydecker

Early Morning Routine

I wake up every day at 4:30 in the morning and prowl around the house. It's sort of my walking meditation, or perhaps you would call it my daily constitutional. No one else is awake then, but I cannot sleep through that hour. I have to get up and get a drink of water, scratch a rug, bat around a wadded ball of paper. Then I visit all the beds and see if anyone's awake yet. I really want to go outside, so I meow at the front door a while until someone grumpily lets me out. I police the grounds outside, then pause by the bathroom window and howl a little until someone groggily lets me back in. Than I walk to the back door and meow some more, but by then I'm usually ignored. I know this annoys my family, but since they're not patrolling the property, someone has to do it. Men, women, and children can afford to be careless. Cats cannot. Our very lives depend on knowing everything at all times.

Finally, around 6:00 A.M., I leap onto the bed of my choosing, turn in a circle, and fall into a deep sleep until everyone else wakes up for the day.

—Mack

Company

Human visitors scare the whiskers out of me. At the same time, I can't help being excruciatingly curious about them. This must be what an addiction is like, to be uncontrollably drawn toward something that is obviously dangerous. When the front door opens, I bolt away. Then I creep toward the newcomer until he spots me. Then I streak away again. I know better than to get near the person, but I feel my legs pulling me toward him just the same. After a while, I stop running away and I might even touch my nose to his shoe. I might eventually let him pet me, too. If addiction is bad for you, then why does it have to feel so good?

—Pooh, age 12

Where to Look for Us
When We're Hiding on Purpose

Suitcase

Top shelf in hall closet

Stack of newspapers

Third dining chair on left of table

Cardboard VCR box in basement

Kitchen cupboard among frying pans

Behind the sofa

Potato bin

Sock drawer that is slightly ajar

Travel carrier (risky!)

Bathtub

—Sheba

Whose Footsteps These Are,
I Think I Know

I sit at the front door, listening to the neighbors walking by our apartment. There's Mrs. Ferraro on her daily shuffle to the stoop. And little Juanita Juarez, who just turned seven, dragging her bicycle outside. Juanita's aunt once stabbed her mother in the leg, and there was a great commotion in the hallway with the police. I can hear the meter reader pausing on the stairway landing to light a cigarette.

Lunchtime arrives. Deliveries are made. Chinese food, Fed Ex, the postal carrier with his jangling keys. As the sun goes down, cars start to honk outside, and the residents come slumping home from work. Chad the ad man, who types his novel every night on his hushed keyboard upstairs. Bert the super, who's not supposed to know I live here.

From faraway, outside, I think I hear the click of a certain Kenneth Cole stacked heel. I reach out my paw and press it against the door, concentrating on the approaching sound. *Cluck, cluck, cluckety cluck.* Yes, I think I'd know that step anywhere. *Cluck, cluck, cluckety cluck.* It's getting closer! I sit up and swivel my ears toward the street door downstairs. A pause, a turn of the key, a shuffle—it's her! I know it is! I call down to her.

"Meow!" I shout through the door, as she checks the mailbox. "I'm up here—all alone!"

She calls back: "I hear you! Hi, sweetie!"

She sounds a little casual. But I am so excited! I stand back so the door won't knock me over when she opens it. I hear her high heels coming up the stairs. She's unlocking the door! I turn in a circle and check my fur, then sit up straight with an upturned look of adoring expectation. She comes in and swoops down to hug me. The days are long with worry, but when I'm in her arms, I am the luckiest cat in the world.

—Cookie

When Cats Were King

In ancient Egypt, cats were treated with great respect. Not lions or tigers or leopards, but simple little cats. They were worshipped by humans. They were served fresh chopped liver on golden plates. They inspired mammoth sphinx sculptures. They rode in chauffeured chariots. They were buried in great pyramids. They wore gold earrings. They were the coolest animals on the planet.

Thousands of years later, no one lives in pyramids anymore, and chariots are a thing of the past. But the essence of a cat's power over humans hasn't changed. I say let's start a movement to remind every cat that he (or she) is almighty and powerful. Let's bring back the single gold earring as a symbol of our pride. Jewelry is expensive, true, but it was ever so. I'll be the first cat to wear one. Then more will join me. When you see a cat wearing an earring, you will know us. And we'll know ourselves.

I am cat. Hear me roar.

— Raj

Love

It is so easy to give people love. They are so helpless and ugly. No fur, no paws, no tail. They run away from mice. They never get enough sleep. How can you help but love such an absurd animal?

Cats are better cats when they love humans. This becomes crystal clear when you meet a cat who has no people, like Victor. Victor built his own house out of an old barn. He has way too many children, more than he can handle. He has diseases and fleas, and sometimes he steals my food, my girlfriend, and my favorite snoozing spot under the morning glory. He thinks humans are awful. He won't go near any of them. And, by now, few humans want to go near Victor anyway, although some still try.

Victor's not happy. And somewhere a human is less happy because she has no cat to love her. Life is filled with strange ironies. But, right now, I need a nibble and a nap. I'll continue this thought tomorrow.

—Hudson

Dignity

One time I leaped onto a bed, and the satin comforter was so slippery I fell back down the side of the bed and landed on my elbow. Of course, I sat straight up immediately, frowned, and flattened my ears to half-mast. This made me look cool and collected, so anyone who might have seen me fall would think I was just practicing my back flip. Then I licked my arm and jogged over to the bedroom closet to investigate an imaginary sound.

It's not easy recovering from a slipup, especially when you're a cat. It's even worse when a person sees you do it. As a cat, you are expected to make perfect leaps, vaults, and somersaults and stick your landing every time. When people manage to achieve this, crowds cheer and sing and award gold medals; then they put the leaper's face on cereal boxes. For a cat, it's considered ordinary and ho-hum, yet woe to the cat who falters, even for an instant.

My friend Grizzly told me about the time she leapt to her usual post on the toilet lid to watch her dad take a shower. Only this time, her dad forgot to put the lid down, and she landed in the bowl. It was a humiliating error, and she was also soaking wet. A cat's nightmare. There is no way you can pretend you meant to jump into a toilet. Grizzly panicked and tried to claw her way out of the big white bowl. She slid and splashed again. She gave a little yelp. A cat in water is like a fish out of water. A cat who is not dry and fluffy and proud is not a cat at all.

When her dad emerged from the shower and found Grizzly, licking and shaking in the bedroom, he did the best possible thing a person can do. He dried her off and set Grizzly carefully on his bed. And then he never mentioned it to her again. And he never mentioned it to anyone else, either.

This is what good people do.

— *Woody*

The Symbols of Slumber Formation

When a cat curls up to nap, he or she will form a different shape every time. One day she might look like a football, another time a perfect circle, some days a sort of L-shape, and even, sometimes, all stretched out like a rocking horse on its side.

People have long wondered what determines the attitude a sleeping cat will assume. Some think we curl up in order to resemble a snake, just like when we hiss and flatten our ears to scare away our enemies. But the truth is much more simple. We curl up to form a smile. We don't all have lips that smile, but we all have bodies that do. So even when we're not feeling our best, it doesn't have to show to the outside world. We can just curl up into a large smile—wide, small, open, closed—whatever our mood.

When Alice went through the looking glass, she saw the smile of the Cheshire Cat, which remained after the cat itself had disappeared. Let me ask you this: What do you think Alice really saw? Was it a smile, or was it a cat—or was it *a smile and a cat?* I leave you to ponder this yourself. Yours truly,

—Fluffball

Vinnie's Nine Niftiest
Food Substitutions

Lizard = 1 chipmunk + 1 praying mantis

Moth = 1 housefly + dust from under the bed + water

Or: 3 spiders

Vole = 1 mouse or 2 baby moles

Turtle = 1 fish + 1 june bug

Grass = 3 tulips from a crystal vase

Milk = water, dripping directly from faucet only

Fish = crunchy dead leaves

Catnip = dirt + debris from human's shoe treads

Vomit = 1 can generic cat food from Slim's Pharmacy

Warning: Do not use cockroaches, roses, or ants in any culinary combination.

The Scent of Another

Sometimes when my person comes home from an outing, I am shocked to discover evidence that he has been with another cat. I can always tell. I'll walk by his discarded sneakers and uncover the telltale hairs of an unknown rival. I'll smell the shoes attentively, then glare at him in an attempt to get him to confess. He always does, eventually.

Once, I found the scent of another cat when he brought home a library book. I sniffed at the pages and looked up at him with a frown. He swore backwards and forwards that he himself had not been with a cat, but that the *book* must have been with a cat in someone else's home. I looked at the book. It had a watercolor painting of a cat on the front. It actually looked like a good read, if there really is such a thing. I rubbed my cheek against the edge of the cover. The foreign scent faded a little. I rubbed the book again, a little harder this time. It felt good. Soon the book took on the scent of me.

My best advice for coping with the scent of another

cat is to drown the offending scent with your own unique perfume. Not the Paco Rabanne in the bathroom, but the scent you carry in your cheekbones. You can't bottle that, baby.

—*Frenchie*

How to Open a Sliding Screen Door

No cat likes to see a closed door. However, when a door is closed, it usually means there is something good to eat on the other side. Rather than get depressed about encountering a closed door, how about empowering yourself to do something and beginning to conquer the obstacles in your life?

Research has shown that new door technology, here at the dawn of the twenty-first century, makes it more and more difficult for a cat to break down these annoying barriers. But every cat should know there is one door that will yield to the power of your positive thinking. Tell yourself you can do it, over and over again. Then walk to your nearest sliding screen door.

Sit in front of the sliding door. Sniff to see if the glass part has been moved aside. If you smell grass, you're halfway there.

Using your strongest arm, raise your paw and sink your claws into the screen at about shoulder level. Take a deep breath. Then, slowly grasping the screen with your claws, use your biceps to slide the door in one direction. If it doesn't budge, try pushing in the other direction. When the door starts to move, keep pushing with your claws in that same direction. In only a few seconds, you will have enough clearance to squeeze through to the outdoors.

It seems difficult at first, but once you get the routine down, it becomes easier. Some cats prefer to develop a small hole in the screen with their claws. Before long, you can nose through this small hole like a companionway. You have made your own pet door within the screen! However, you have also provided an entry to intruders. Sometimes they are edible, but not always. The price of convenience may be too high for you in this matter. Each must decide for himself.

Rather than viewing a closed door as a barrier, look at it as an opportunity to test your hidden strengths. And feel free to call me if you need help.

— *Woody*

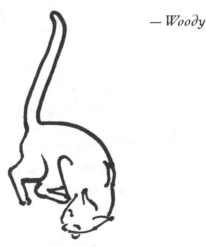

Cats Always Come Back

It's a sad truth that humans, even the ones we love, sometimes go away and never come back. They get killed, or kidnapped, or reassigned to a new home without telling us.

Cats always return. They might be transported hundreds of miles from their homes, but they have the innate sense to go back to where they're from. Humans were not born with this natural gift. Therefore, it is always up to us to find them, not vice versa. Go to your local shelter and observe the lost humans looking for the faces they love. Even if you do not find the same humans who left you, you will probably find another set who needs you just as badly.

No one can explain why humans lack the homing instinct we felines take for granted. Sometimes an animal can have too much range, I suppose, and too much range is like having no range at all. Do not follow the humans' example in this matter. Provide for them, instead, a model of stability and pride of place. They can learn from you what it means to have a home.

— Tiger

Eavesdropping

People don't know this, because we do it with such stealth and cunning, but cats listen to every word people say. Most of what we hear is forgettable, but some things arouse our curiosity and stick with us. Here are pieces of actual human conversations I've heard. I still ponder these comments from time to time:

"The Martins put their cat to sleep yesterday."

"I can't wear my fur tonight—it's in storage."

"Tomorrow we are going to the Vee Eee Tee."

"The Jamesons have a new black Cadillac."

"Brian let the cat out of the bag."

"They sailed a catamaran to Jamaica."

"There's more than one way to skin a cat."

"The cat's got his tongue."

"Tell her I'm not here."

—Portia

Vinnie's Nine Niftiest
Funny People Activities to Watch

1. Vacuuming
2. Getting dressed in the morning
3. Having sex
4. Taking a shower or bath
5. Talking on the telephone
6. Waking up when the alarm goes off
7. Doing aerobics in the living room
8. Shaving
9. Playing basketball

Remembrance of Things Past

Not long ago I discovered my human mother scratching her fingernails with a little piece of sandpaper. Naturally, I found the noise very appealing. So I walked over and sniffed at it. She told me it was an emery board. I watched with interest as she filed a couple of her nails. Then I had this overwhelming desire to rub my cheek against this thing. I dove at it with my nose. What a sensation! It was the scratchy tongue of my real mother. I took the emery board between my two front paws and rubbed it on one side of my face, then the other. I couldn't stop! It was something I hadn't felt in years! Mom! Mom! I purred and rubbed some more. Visions of my birth mother soothing me with her tongue came back to me.

An emery board . . . isn't it funny the odd thing that will trigger such important memories for a cat?

—Punk

Cleanliness Is Godliness

It's amazing to me how easy I am to clean and how difficult it is for people to clean anything. I remember the time I spilled a big bottle of black ink on the yellow carpet and, of course, all over my tawny self. Well, I didn't spill it really. I just saw on the desk a jar that had to go over the side, and the ink just happened to be inside the jar, which I couldn't have known. Not that it would have made any difference.

Anyway, so there I was with black ink all over, even on my paws. I walked in a little circle to make some paw prints on the floor, but before long the magic wore off, and my footprints became invisible again. The cleaning lady came in and squawked and shouted and shook her finger at me. Her finger looked like a baby mouse.

I laid down on the floor and held up my two front paws. I looked pretty good in black! But the ink was sticky, so I got down to work licking it off. Meanwhile, the cleaning lady got to work on the yellow carpet with a vile foam spray and a rag. Beads of sweat formed on her forehead, and she muttered things under her breath.

About ten minutes later, my coat was dry and fluffed back to its normal beige. I stretched and yawned. I love being a cat. The cleaning lady threw down her rag and marched out of the room. I glanced over at the floor. The carpet was still unsightly. Splotches of purple on yellow—she had only made the mess look worse.

How come the cleaning person is so much larger than I am, with a much bigger tongue, and yet she can't remove a simple stain from a natural fiber? People never clean things well. What enzyme is missing from their saliva? And if they're so bad at cleaning things, how come they still make dirt everywhere they go? I never make a mess I can't clean up myself. If they're not going to get the hang of cleaning up, then people should simplify their lifestyles and bring less dirt into their lives.

— *Virgil*

Big Dumb Cats

All humans are, of course, giant cats. They are not
very smart, but are lovably ugly, without much in the
way of ears or hair. They are young cats, unrefined by
time, poor hunters with weak nails and flat mouths.
But there appears to be a more evolved human, one
who has pointed teeth and loves to hiss. They hunt
during the night, carnivores who kill their prey with a
swift bite to the neck. That is the human they call
"vampire."

They sleep in big boxes during the day, maintain an
impeccably groomed appearance, slink around at night
from pillar to post, yet vampires have never been con-
nected to the feline world by the dull-witted human. If
anything, humans believe vampires evolved from *bats*.
I ask you. Clearly this proves that the human is blind
to his true origins.

Although you and I can see which humans are vampires, I recommend we keep this information to ourselves. Humans get all riled up if they suspect a vampire
is in their midst. When you see a vampire, you are free

to signal a greeting by yawning wide, flashing him or her your fangs. But no more than that. They are the humans closest to cats, and we want to keep their evolution in motion.

—*Sherman*

A Spoonful of Tuna Oil
with That, Please

I have a slight pancreas problem. Who knew? So now
I have to take special medication. Every day I get pills
shoved down my throat. Somebody jams a finger
between my jaws and—*bam!*—he pops one in there. I
get my tongue working immediately to stop it from
going down my throat. If I catch it, I hide the pill in my
gums for as long as I can. I quietly spit it into a corner
and look at it for a few moments. Then, I sweep it
under the rug with my paw. If someone sees me doing
this, I quickly attack the rug like there's a big rat under
there. The observer usually shrugs and leaves me
alone.

Then I head outdoors for a homeopathic dose of
echinacea, sage, and catnip. I roll around on the grass
and let a chive tickle my nose. Ah, the healing power of
nature! My pancreas is feeling fine, thank you.

— Woody

Curiosity

People like to say curiosity killed the cat. But a cat already knows everything there is to know and has already met everyone he ever needs to meet. Much as people like to believe it, curiosity is simply not a pronounced cat trait. Cats are more likely to die from a courageous act, human error, untimely virus, or speeding car.

In fact, I would say curiosity has killed plenty more people than it has cats. Man's insatiable desire to know what's at the top of a Himalayan peak, to experience a free fall in the sky, to drive a car really fast, to water-ski behind a motorboat, to run twenty-six miles without stopping, to ride the Zipper, to take hallucinogenic drugs, to snowboard down a mountain—these are things a cat is not curious about in the least. In fact, we are hardly curious that people are so taken with such bizarre activities. We prefer the safe routine, the dependable nourishment, napping, grooming, the curiously *noncurious* lifestyle. We don't even like to go to the movies or have our favorite seat occupied temporarily by a houseguest.

Don't get me started on who's curious and who's not. Don't even get me started.

—Bisu

Vinnie's Nine Niftiest Pounces

1. Silent vault to top of bookcase
2. Chair-to-kitchen-table double leg
3. Startled four-paw, straight-up rocket blast-off
4. Swan dive from second step of back deck to chipmunk hole
5. Headlock on moving toes under bedspread
6. Breast stroke through pile of newspapers
7. Air Jordan to imaginary bird in backyard
8. Bounce off a carpeted wall
9. *Lord of the Dance* two-legged jig around cheese tray on coffee table

Newton's Law

When I was a kit, I was constantly knocking beverage glasses off tables. I couldn't help it—a part of me just had to see what happened when a container filled with liquid fell to the floor. It was never the same twice!

Suppose there is a small glass of orange juice on the kitchen table. You go up and push it with your paw until it goes over the edge. A tiny glass of juice makes a horrible crash, with flying glass everywhere and satisfying screams from the humans, and I have to leap away into a distant corner for a while.

On the other hand, mosey over to a big bottle of mineral water sitting on the coffee table. It's really heavy, so you can't just move it with your paw. You have to press your nose down near the bottom of the bottle and bulldoze it off the table. A muffled galugg—and that's all! You get down to look at the bottle—nothing is broken, the water is still inside, and the people didn't even hear it fall! Water is obviously not as explosive as orange juice.

I spent years doing such experiments until I finally grew too old to leap on tables. This meant I had to retire from my career as a physicist. However, there is one spot where an old tinkerer like me can still get in a good shove: the nightstand.

Lying quietly in bed around four or five o'clock in the morning is really a challenge for me. Not long ago, I discovered that a good use for this dark hour is clearing off the bedside table one object at a time.

Lying next to the pillow at the edge of my bed, I can see everything on top of the nightstand, even in total darkness. I reach a paw out to those folded eyeglasses on the nightstand. Pretty, reflective glass. Light as a feather. Off they go! Muffled plop onto the carpet. I hate carpet. Carpet should be put on walls, not floors. The falling eyeglasses don't even wake anyone up. Try the small book. It's heavier than it looks. Audubon bird guide. Birds! Gotta go. Two paws for this effort. Aargh! Did it! Boom! Slight rise from the bed.

"Woody, will you cut it out!"

What else is on the table? Telephone, clock, bottle of water. Well, I know the water won't do anything exciting. Let's try the clock. It's big, but not difficult to move with just a flick of the wrist. Wham! It banks off the wall before landing on the rug.

"Woodddiiiieeee!"

Adrenaline soars. I am a raging lion. Let's go for the phone, big guy.

It weighs a little more, but with two paws and a fat shove with the nose, it's sailing. Three rings, a crash, a bounce, and a spiraling loose bolt skitters over to the wood floor. A dark head peers over the side of the bed and groans.

Three points, Wood Man. You made the Final Four for this year's Nobel Prize.

— Woody

Warm-Ups

No cat gets moving in the morning without a few stretches. In fact, every time we wake up is a good time to stretch. Some cats might like to exercise in a group, but I find it easier to just stay at home and work out alone. Here's what I do:

The Hokey-Pokey Stretch: Place your left paw forward, claws outstretched, as if you were going to rake some leaves like a human. Reach so far that your back forms a "U," with your rear end high in the air. You should be reaching so far that your whole body vibrates with tension. Now, repeat with your right paw. Reach! Pretend a mouse is a mile away and you're going to get it with one swipe. Now, reach with both paws straight out front together. Press your armpits to the floor. Open the claws wide as they scrape the floor. Feel the pull on your hamstrings. Doesn't that feel great?

The Circus Seal Stretch: This one works on your chest and rear leg muscles. With all four paws on the floor, lift one hind leg slightly and stretch it straight back like Nureyev in *The Nutcracker*. Hold, perfectly straight, for three seconds. Then put your leg down and lift the other hind leg. Stretch straight as if your leg is a bridge over a wide river!

Now, using your front arms, pull your chest up and forward, stretching both legs out behind you. Drag your ankles as if you're a sea lion. You are a land lion! The Circus Seal Stretch is terrific for groin muscles and obliques.

Begin each waking period with this series of stretches and you will get the adrenalin flowing. Warm up all your muscles so you don't experience the strain, stiffness, and backaches that plague tense humans all the time.

Whatever your age or size, find a regime that works for you and stick to it. A cat has never been injured due to flexibility or prowess. Let's keep it that way.

—Moose

New Cat Values

Ninety-nine percent of all cats never know their fathers. This leaves mom with a lot of children in a single-parent household. Not only that, but she has precious little time—only a few weeks—to prepare these kitties for the road of life.

For this reason, and due to the relatively recent invention of birth control, fewer and fewer cats are choosing to be stay-at-home moms.

We applaud this trend and we are working to make it easier for a cat to choose the lifestyle she wants. We are here for any support you require on your path to independence.

—Drs. Whiskers, Bradish & McCarthy,

Cats' Alliance to Legalize
Independent Cat Options
(CALICO)

Getting Free Stuff

The secret to happiness is to get free stuff. And your key to getting free stuff is right in the pad of your paw. It's not about money, fur color, education, or bloodline. It's about attitude — and looking good.

All you need to do to get free stuff is to pose very cutely, preferably against a background that best contrasts your natural hair color. Here's an example: Shadow is black and her hair is short. She knows she looks prettiest against the lavender satin armchair under the orchid. When she needs an hors d'oeuvre, or just a human rub-down, she lies on her back, with all four paws in the air, and hangs her head over the side of the cushion upside down. She blinks her wide eyes at everyone who walks by. And they never just walk by.

It doesn't take long before half the family is praising her beauty and rewarding her outward charm with snacks and hugs. Now, you and I know that Shadow is a selfish tattletale who hit her brother James when he was only three days old. But she has a heck of a talent for getting free stuff. Take a lesson, my fellow cats. She's a mean one, but she knows how to be happy.

—Nickleby

The Secret Language of Tails

Bottlebrush bristles, straight up at ninety degrees:
    "Not funny!"

Curving down to the floor as gently as a playground slide:
    "It wasn't me!"

Question mark:
    "How do I look?"

Windshield wiper swishing and swashing:
    "Attention! Attention! There is a mouse in this room."

Curled around reposed body:
    "I love me. Don't you?"

Metronome whomping on the floor:
    "You'd better stop teasing me, or I'll kill you!"

Thad and Maude

They are not married and they are not siblings by blood, but they live together as a family. They came from different birthplaces they would just as soon put far behind them—Thaddeus from the shelter; Maude from a box outside the car dealership. Now they live together with some humans in Evanston.

They don't look alike. Thad is black tuxedo with a white patch on every extremity, including his nose. Maude is a long-haired redhead who has to get shaved every summer because her hair is too high maintenance, even with her and Thad both working it together.

Thaddeus and Maude are platonic friends, roommates, a makeshift adoptive family, as is becoming more common in America. They were forced together, not like a Moonie marriage, but in a rare friendship forged from mutual respect, a common sense of humor, and a zest for good grooming.

— *Woody*

Every Hour of the Day
Take a Moment Just for Play

Cats know not to take life too seriously. Nothing is too important to put down and goof off for a while. Not many creatures have this gift. The industrious squirrel, the whiny blue jay, the workhorse and the bassett hound just plod along; if the world ended tomorrow, that would be fine with them.

Cats never feel this way. And this is how you can tell. Watch Kitty for a while. Watch her sleep, meditate, meet another cat, or drink some water. Very little time will pass in her serious endeavor before she will leap at the wall, slip and slide on an area rug, or bat a Hershey's Kiss around the floor like a hockey puck. Sometimes she'll be walking along, and then suddenly tear around the room at lightning speed. Then she stops and flattens her ears like she hardly knows what hit her.

Cats know that every life requires a little excitement. Not too much, mind you, but something to blow the hair back every once in a while. If humans do not provide the occasional thrill of the chase, cats will invent one for themselves. We are our own best company!

— Pepper

My Weekly Diary

Monday   Wake up, clean my belly, patrol the house, snack, wash my face, nap on living room chair, social hour with humans, dinner, TV, nap, snack, bedtime.

Tuesday   Wake up, snack, go outdoors, observe garbage pick-up, taste crunchy debris on garage floor, nap under wheel cover, go inside for lunch. Nap on pile of dry cleaning, snack, scratch rugs, stare out window at imaginary birds, dinner, read newspaper, snack, bed.

Wednesday Backyard pinecone softball, torture eight-ounce mouse, eat all but head, deposit head on doormat, lick Mom, nap, lunch, all-over body cleansing, dinner, chase Dad's shoelaces, sneak lap time when no one is looking, nap, snack, bedtime.

Thursday   Climb oak tree, watch kids gather around tree, observe Mr. Mays bring out a ladder and climb up my tree. Chew on leaves, listen to everyone cheering my name, nap, clean ribcage and forearms, climb down tree, escape human grasps, lunch. Nap, dinner, couch time, snack, bed.

Friday   Wake up, patrol house, snack, wash my ears, nap on towel on bathroom floor, stretch, watch vacuum cleaner, lunch, nap, sit on window sill and listen to soap operas, snack, cocktail hour with bacon-wrapped cheese balls, dinner, bath time, nap, snack, bed.

Saturday   Rake backyard, nip Mr. Mays from beneath his hammock, pounce practice, afternoon mouse roast, shower, nap, snack, dinner, tummyache, wary hour on haunches in living room waiting to vomit, nap, midnight patrol, snack, chase shadows in kitchen.

Sunday   Dawn wake-up call for household, pancake breakfast, kill newspapers, nap, lunch, nap, clean tail and surrounding area, observe litter change, raise paw to request more dirt, nod approval, snack, dinner, nap, snack, bed.

—Seneca

The Ghosts of Those
Who Went Before

Ever see a cat looking really hard at something, but you cannot see what it is they are focusing on?

I am one of those animals who sees the ghosts of dogs and cats who used to play in my neighborhood many years ago. Even after they grow old and die, they never really leave the block. They're still playing in their favorite places, well, okay, their old haunts, if you will.

Barney the mutt still cruises down by the river looking for fish and never catching any. Jake the spaniel is barking at Trevor the shepherd mix on the other side of his old fence. Sherman the angora is sharpening his claws on the black oak.

No one can see them but me. I don't mind. It's a little less lonely this way. How can I tell the ghosts from my living neighbor pets? Well, for starters, you can see through the ghosts, of course. Plus, they don't make any noise. No woofs, mews, or yelps come out of their moving lips.

Don't feel sad if a member of your household passes on. She's still right there next to you, panting bad breath, as always. And your surviving cat is watching over her.

— *Fuzzy*

Vinnie's Nine Niftiest Ways to Assess a Strange Human's Character

1. Wink at the person. If he winks back, he's cool. If not, then congratulations! You have just given that person the heebie-jeebies and asserted your power over him.

2. Smell the stranger's shoes. If she pulls away from you, she has something to hide. If she bends over right away to pet you, she has a rival pet she feels guilty about hiding. If she stares at you and doesn't know how to react, she is unused to cats and needs guidance from you.

3. Meow at the person. If he does nothing, he is afraid of you. If he meows back, he has no cat at home and thinks this is how a person should speak to a cat. If he answers your query in normal human English, like "Thank you, Chester, it's nice to meet you too," or "No thanks, I just had lunch," then he has utmost repect for you and is worthy of your trust.

4. Rub against the stranger's legs. This divides the strong from the weak. If she rubs you back, she is truly nice and wants to get to know you better. If she pulls away, then you are a cougar in her eyes.

Play it up, then. Hiss and snarl a little. Be the cougar she thinks you are!

5. Hop on Mom's lap and put your butt near her face, keeping your eyes on the stranger at all times. This shows the visitor you are marking your territory, that Mom belongs to you, not to him. If you see the visitor put his butt near your mom's face, then you have lost her forever, or at least for a while.

6. Sit under the TV set while a basketball game is on and talk to the stranger. If he talks back to you, then he does not really like basketball and should be ignored. If he ignores you to watch the game, then go over and enjoy the visitor's lap.

7. Give a nip at the visitor's elbow. A wimpy human will cry out as if you'd just cut off her arm. A playful, friendly human will simply nip you back.

8. Cough a lot, like you're going to toss a hair ball. Inch toward the visitor's shoes, rasping for breath. Rest your chin on her loafer. If she's frozen like a garden statue, attack her ankles, and I guarantee she'll scream.

9. Attempt to sit on the visitor's lap. Genital shyness means he has something to hide.

Reach Out and Touch

Sometimes when my human is talking to me, he calls it "talking on the phone." There's no one else in the room, and all of a sudden he'll say, "I'm talking on the phone, Bean," then proceed to laugh and gossip and tell me all the stories about his day. Naturally, I respond in kind. I rub up against the telephone and speak into the receiver, too. I'm not sure why he likes to play this plugged-in chitchat game, but it pleases me to hear him so bubbly. He's not always this warm and lively when he's alone with me. When he talks to me with his telephone and shares the details of his life with me, I know how much he truly loves me.

— Bean

Earthquakes

My job during an earthquake is to hold the floor together. I spread my four paws as far apart as they will go, I dig in with my nails, and hang on for the ride. It looks like surfing on a wave, except sometimes the floor bumps my chin, or my belly button gets a rug burn.

My ancestors came to North America on a giant ship from China, and this is how I was born with natural sea legs. They have served me well in California. And thus far, I have kept my house from falling down on several occasions. I am quite powerful. And cute. Needless to say, I am the most important member of the household.

—Sunshine

Turning Gray and Going Deaf

Many cats grow deaf and gray as they get old, although some cats are born gray, and most white cats with blue eyes are deaf their whole lives. But growing old is not that bad for a cat. In fact, as cats age, we become more human.

We stop leaping like kittens. We watch more television. We eater softer foods. We belch after lunch, and sometimes we even get the hiccups. We add a couple naps to the daily agenda. We use ramps, when available, more often than stairs. We move our nesting spots closer to the litter box for convenience. Our grandchildren drift away from us. We develop bladder control problems. But we try to keep that to ourselves and still enjoy outings. We sit closer to the fireplace than ever before. We sit silently and smile a lot, so that others won't be concerned about us.

I learned a lot about aging gracefully from humans. I hope they learn some things from me, too.

—Hopi

Vinnie's Nine Niftiest
Travel Tips

1. Help your person pack more economically—sit in the suitcase.

2. Always get others to carry your bags.

3. Do not pause to relieve yourself at any station along the way—travel facilities are notoriously unsanitary!

4. Do not stare at strange-looking travelers, but do try to covertly study any French cats whose paths you cross. You always learn something from a French cat.

5. Use your third eyelid frequently to prevent dry eye.

6. Flirt with all flight attendants and gas station guys, and you will get free stuff.

7. You will be welcomed in France, Burma, Persia, Angora, Siam, and Egypt, but you will be hassled in England and Scotland. The State Department recommends, as a safety precaution, that you stay out of China and New Guinea altogether.

8. Rubbing forehead to forehead is the universal language of love.

9. Jet lag will make you cranky, unless you maintain a twenty-hour sleep schedule every day of your entire trip.

Aromatherapy

Sometimes all you need to brighten up your day is a fresh scent that will lift your darker moods. We've seen people pay exorbitant prices for candles, dead flowers, incense, soaps, and bottles of oil. Even a cat can appreciate dead catnip now and then. But a cat knows where to go for the most effective aromatherapy. Outdoors.

Humans haven't yet made the connection that all the artificial scents they purchase exist for real (and for free) in nature. But cats have never forgotten, and this healing treatment is an important element of a cat's regimen.

Going outdoors reminds us of the meaning of life. In winter, cats rub up against the bark of evergreen, tamarack, and birch. Pine sap helps coats stay shiny and waterproof. The blooms of spring and summer provide weeks of pleasure and relaxation—from daffodils and freesia to jasmine and lilac. The smell of fresh muskrats and squirrels reminds us of the cornucopia nature provides a meat eater.

Tell your people to stop being fooled by the promises of artificial scents. Take your loved one for a walk outside today.

—Button

Party Animal

When my people entertain, I find a variety of ways to enjoy myself. I have tried being the center of attention, which I do effortlessly by sprawling on the living room carpet. But the people usually spill Champagne on my tummy and, in spite of their worship, they never offer even a nibble of their liver pâté or salmon mousse. I used to indulge in ankle-charging some of the humans, which always helped get the dancing started.

Nowadays, I shy away from the crowds in the living room and revel in the best place of all during a human social gathering: on the bed with all the discarded coats.

Okay, so now I'll tell you . . . I am a lifetime wool sucker. I tried to stop myself from this childhood habit, but after middle age I just gave up. Where's the harm, after all? I like to suck on sweaters, coats, hats, and blankets like a kid sucks on his useless thumb. And nothing's better than a roomful of coats because, like Goldilocks, I can spend hours testing each one for flavor, texture, and body heat. No one in the other room will ever know unless they come in and find me snoozing on my favorite one.

Some wool coats are prickly, which I can never understand because sheep don't have a prickly part on their entire bodies. It's as though shards of glass have been added to the coat fabric. Those coats I steer clear of.

Angora is a nice addition to wool—the Angora cat in me recalls the Angora goats and rabbits, and the sensation of angora in wool sends me back to my previous lives in Turkey.

The furs are a little frightening, because one time I encountered a fox I'd met before, when it was alive and well and living in the Hudson River valley. It is the one superstition a cat possesses: He who sits on someone's fur coat will one day *be* someone's fur coat.

Cashmere is the best human coat of all—cashmere coats feel most like cat hair, to me. I have never met the cashmere goat face to face, but I can tell from his hair that he is a most loving animal. I like the red cashmere goat most of all. I get a little spit on him. Sighing with contentment, I fall asleep. I look terrific on red cashmere. I think this party guest should not go home at all.

—Clemenza

Questions We Will Never Know the Answers To, Though We Do Know Everything Else

1. A. What flavor is Nine Lives' "Super Supper"?
   B. If it's so super, how come they don't say what it is?

2. If cats love fish so much, why do we hate to swim?

3. I cannot keep a part in my hair: What gives?

4. If cats are the fairest of them all, why are catfish so ugly?

5. Have we died and gone to heaven—or is catnip really legal?

6. Why do we get all sorts of ailments, but never insomnia?

— Woody

Color Me Beautiful

Some cats need advice on which colors bring out the best in their natural beauty. Your appearance is always impeccable, so it's not important to be overly concerned with how you look, but some humans have a strong reaction to a cat who's in optimal contrast to his surroundings. When you're down or in dire need of dedicated human love, the color wheel might help you. Here's a quick chart to refer to when you need to attract positive attention.

If You Are . . .	*Sit or Lie On . . .*
Orange, or orange and white	You are Autumn! Choose slate-colored accents like a gray comforter, white sofa, black, or any shade of blue.
Black, or black and white	Hello, Winter! You are best lying contrasted by warm tones of red, gold satin, and beige knits!

Gray (solid or tabby)	The cool Spring cat with his charcoal pinstripes looks best against red, white, lavender, or light blue.
Calico	Our Summer gal looks best in white, pink, or yellow. Not many cats can get away with these colors!

—Carole

Litter Box Boogie

Cats prefer the great outdoors when it comes to most bodily functions. But there are situations—indeed, for some cats their entire lives—when nature is unavailable to us. Imagine the city cat who never gets to roll in grass!

I have some thoughts on how humans could best re-create the w. c. *en plein air* which, for many cats, has gone the way of the sabertooth. They're small things, perhaps, to some, but vitally important to an immaculate cat.

1. Fresh dirt, as often as possible, please. The sand stuff is okay, but it tracks throughout the house and I'm not crazy about that. The old-fashioned "kitty litter" is easier to shake off my feet.

2. It is unclear to me why humans put a lid on the litter box. What was once a corner of simulated nature has now become a crude shack under a carbon filter. It's like a reversion to outhouse days. The box lid is so unnatural, you might as well teach me how to go on a human potty. Please remove the lid.

3. Sometimes, in emergencies only, I need to drag my butt behind me for a few yards. I prefer the living room carpet for this purpose. Do not attempt to buy me special mats and rugs to place around the litter box. They're too small for me, and besides they get in the way of the post-box dig-and-rake ritual. You've heard that "Employees must wash hands before leaving washroom"? Well, "Cats must dig and scratch before departing litter area." Bare floors around the box, please. We'll make it to the living room if we need extra personal cleaning assistance.

4. Privacy is important, but I have seen homes where the cat's toilet box was put in the dampest corner of the basement, next to spider webs and oil tanks and dessicated old mops. Would you care to visit such a place several times a day? Imagine how it would affect your digestive patterns. Elimination is not a pretty element of life, but please don't go out of your way to make it downright unpleasant.

5. A window to look through would give me something to do while I'm there. Or at least a picture to look at. A pin-up calendar. That's all.

—*Einstein*

Canned Food Flavors We Know Must Exist, but We Cannot Find

1. Mouse
2. Canary and egg
3. Rabbit
4. Chipmunk
5. Catnip and cream
6. Squirrel with gravy
7. Goldfish entree
8. Shrew and giblets
9. Pig intestines

Toys We Love

Smart people know we play with silly cat toys just to be polite. As if we can't tell the difference between a bit of cardboard and wire and a real moth! We try to send people the message by hiding these toys under the furniture as quickly as possible, or by placing one of those bell things right in the hallway so they poke their feet in the middle of the night. Some of us are lucky to have people who really understand what kind of artificial prey might interest us.

Patsy has a human who once bought her a remote-control toy truck. She was somewhat amused by it, but it smelled lousy and didn't shriek much. She lost interest after a few minutes, and went to clean her face in the hall corner. In the middle of her task, the toy truck squealed past her, and this time there was something irresistably different about it. Patsy looked up and watched the truck careen into the dining room. In its little rear customized flatbed was a giant bowl of fresh turkey! The truck was a big shrieking bird!

Patsy chased the truck all over the house. She grabbed it and grasped it with both arms and took a big chunk of meat into her teeth. It was warm and juicy! She was so enamored with the fresh turkey that the truck leaped out of her arms and raced into the kitchen. Patsy licked her chops and looked around for the truck. She crept into the kitchen.

It was alive again—even though she'd eaten part of it! It was still charging around the house with warm meat for her to catch! She chased that darn truck until she couldn't run anymore and all the meat was gone.

Have you ever heard of a cooler man-made toy? I shake my head to think about it. That Patsy is one lucky cat.

—Nipsy

Give Me Paws

Communicating with people can be a cat's biggest challenge. It's impossible to tell them when we have a tummyache, a hangnail, or a general sense of loneliness. They have a far easier time communicating their frustrations to us. Nothing is more eloquent than the tears of a human.

When a person cries, it is apparent to every cat that the human needs a kiss and a hug right away. I always go over to my person and say, "Are you okay?" I press my paw to her cheek (claws well in check!), look into her eyes, and then I nuzzle her ear. This always makes her feel better. She always hugs me back and thanks me for my concern. I do my part to help because, after all, this galoot of a gangly human is the most important thing in my life.

I have been unable to re-create the tears she employs so well. When I want her to comfort me, I have learned an alternative signal. I raise my paw, claws in, and extend it toward her forearm or her cheek. This gets her attention right away. When she looks at me, I speak, and she appears to listen. If she ignores me, I raise my paw again, as if to say, "No, really, this is important, please pay attention." The second time she will usually listen to me in earnest. I talk a little, tell her about my tummyache, and when I'm done speaking, she'll coo and hug me. This always makes me feel better!

When you want them to really listen, simply raise your right or left paw. They understand this means "stop." Then you can cry all you want to, and they'll lick your tears, too

— *Taxi*

Moments in History
When a Cat Could Have Made a Big Difference

1. Signing of the Declaration of Independence. All those delicate, scrolled John Hancocks and not a solid paw print anywhere. It looks like a pretty wimpy declaration, and considering it was independence they were declaring, it is sorely lacking the endorsement of someone who knows what independence is.

2. Invention of the telephone by Alexander Graham Bell. A cat's meow to Dr. Watson might have changed the entire nature of telephone etiquette.

3. 1998 NBA Playoffs. Cat on boards takes Jordan by surprise. Air ball. Pacers win playoffs, then take championship.

— Ophelia

Tail Size

In this day and age of humility and economy, there are still, unfortunately, cats who get carried away by the size of their own tails. The bigger his tail, the more important the cat thinks he is. Rather than rely on feline grace and charm, Raccoon, the la-dee-dah Maine Coon, can act like a jerk. But because he waves his tail, no human is the wiser.

Some say it isn't the quantity, it's the quality. But I daydream about seeing that long tail clipped by a heavy door. Or a dog who chomps it to a permanently embarrassing angle.

One day, I went upstairs and knocked a bucket of water out the window onto Raccoon. You know what? His glorious tail was reduced to a veritable earthworm. In reality, Raccoon's wet tail was smaller than mine.

Not that size matters, of course.

—Muggsy

You Can Buy a Cat,
but You Can't Bribe One

I live with an old sheepdog named Shep. As you can imagine, the household is awash in his hair, which he keeps in a constant state of dishevelment simply to annoy me. To rub my fur the wrong way, so to speak. I have learned, over the years, to let this go. It's not worth the high blood pressure to be fretting over Shep's grooming habits (or lack thereof). Instead, I use him as a daily reminder to keep myself clean and pristine. In this way, I have identified Shep's reason for being. And he is grateful to know it.

Rather than be embarrassed by his dirty hair, Shep seems almost proud of it. Just like he's always proud of getting lots of treats from our family. And this is typical of a dog. For he does that dog thing that a cat will never, ever do: Beg.

This dog will plead, whine, sit up, roll over, pant, drool, and even bark on command. For some reason, humans think this subservient behavior is admirable and should be rewarded. I think it is pathetic. I cannot imagine stooping to such tactics for a lousy piece of old rawhide. A cat takes the higher road—doing the exact opposite of what a human tells her. Walking away as if I didn't care about a treat. Cleaning my face as if there was nothing I wanted to do more. Sure, dog, go beg for your bone. You are a bonehead. I am a goddess.

— Pumpkin

In My Next Life

I asked a number of cats what they would choose to be if they had to come back in another life as a different creature. I told them they couldn't be a cat. Here is a sampling of their replies:

PUFF: I would come back as a human, so I could take a shower and sing and discover why people are addicted to this dangerous activity.

SOCKS: I would have to be myself again, for there is nothing I would rather be.

ISABEL: I would come back as a jaguar. These are huge felines—supercats, really—who get to eat large birds, raccoons, and deer. Laws protect them from being shot by people, and super claws protect them from being eaten by everyone else.

—Siècle

Scars Tell the Story

Some of us have permanent reminders of how brave we have been at certain points in our lives. I lost an eyeball in the infamous Alley Battle of '95. Mimi lost her earlobe to a greyhound. Archie has a permanent hip injury from racing a Ferrari up his driveway.

It's not that we like to hurt ourselves, nor are we simply foolish. We are very enthusiastic and sometimes we have no idea that the activity we're about to embark on will result in excruciating pain. But, you see, we don't even feel it. We have gusto. Get some gusto for yourself and give it a try. You will not believe the things you can do!

—Meringue

What's Wrong with This Picture?

Whenever I walk into a room, I know my human has changed something on purpose to test my inscrutability. It might be slight—an earring on the dresser, a Kleenex on the floor. It might be so great as to be overlooked—the closet door is open when it was closed before. It is part of the game of life to enter a situation and find out what about it is not the same. This element of surprise and discovery makes the blood course faster through my veins! It is the kitty radar, the cat's compass, that brings new wonder to each day.

I police the room. I pause and sniff at the usual suspects. When I have found the interloping washcloth or pencil, I sit next to it and shout, "Found it!" She will shake her head and worship me a little. Scratch my cheeks. More, please! Thank you. Can't wait for tomorrow! Now I'll move on to the kitchen and see what's new in there.

Isn't life fun?

—*Cleo, Queen of Everything*

Maturity Chart

Contrary to human opinion, cats do not age every year the equivalent of seven human years. This is ludicrous and oversimplified. It's true that a human takes much longer to evolve, socially and intellectually, than a cat does. Humans spend far more of their lives passing through childhood and adolescence—nearly twenty years! Humans remain juveniles throughout a cat's lifetime. Imagine! Here's a more realistic comparison chart, as well as a summary of typical age-specific endeavors. It may help you distinguish the true seasons of a cat's life.

Cat Age	Interests	Corresponding Human Age	Interests
6 months	killing real mice	10 years	skateboards, Barbie dolls
8 months	sex	13 years	Star Wars computer games, bicycles
12 months	parenthood	15 years	cargo pants, flirting
2 years	grandchildren	24 years	first job
4 years	sterilization	32 years	children
6 years	television	40 years	adultery
10 years	urinary tract blockage	56 years	kidney stones
14 years	retirement	72 years	retirement
16 years	snoozing	80 years	naps
20 years	snoozing	100 years	naps

Twelve Fingers, Eight Toes
Still Add Up to Twenty

People forget that cats have only four toes on each rear foot. For some reason, people assume we have five, but we don't. We have five toes only on our front paws. Sometimes, however, an extra digit shows up in our front paws. It is not uncommon to find a kitty with six toes on each front paw. The extra sticks out like an apposable thumb. People sometimes get freaked out by this extra toe, just as they do over the poor guy with no tail.

People have this absurd standard that ten toes and ten fingers is normal. How arbitrary is such judgment? Do not be lured into this veiled bigotry, my feline friends. Thumbs up to our universal acceptance of all, even the narrow-minded human.

—Pericles

You vs. the Man of the House

He will roar if you sit in his favorite chair. Sometimes, he'll simply sit on you, as if you weren't there! The man is always trying to squash you. Watch out.

He wants to sleep next to Mom and never next to you. He will actually sweep you off the bed! He doesn't want you anywhere near Mom!

He leaves his dirty clothes all over the place, but they smell so bad, you never want to curl up and sleep on them! You must, however, leave your scent on these clothes to douse the offensive man fumes.

He never gives you food!

If you so much as play with the shoelaces of his smelly sneakers, he yells at you!

And yet, in private, when no one else can see, he snuggles with you on the couch. Moments later, he inexplicably tosses you aside and calls you a sneaky scoundrel.

He treats us so badly. And still we go back for more! Such is the story of the man who is from Mars and the cat who is from Venus.

—*Lady Jane Gray*

Vinnie's Nine Niftiest
Scratch Sites

1. Leather shoes, any style
2. Rubber shoes, like flip-flops
3. La-Z-Boy chair
4. Textured wallpaper in hall
5. Living room rug
6. Scratching post
7. Screen door
8. Pine table leg
9. Wicker chair

Your Personal Cat Zodiac

Aries the Ram
March 21–April 19

Bossy

Taurus the Bull
April 20–May 20

Hibernator

Gemini the Twins
May 21–June 20

Party Animal

Cancer the Crab
June 21–July 22

Fraidy Cat

Leo the Lion
July 23–August 22

King of Cats

Virgo the Virgin
August 23–September 22

Critic

Libra the Balance
September 23–October 22

High-Wire Artist

Scorpio the Scorpion
October 23–November 21

Biter

Sagittarius the Archer
November 22–December 21

Scratcher

Capricorn the Goat
December 22–January 20

Chat au Chèvre

Aquarius the Water Bearer
January 21–February 19

Cranky

Pisces the Fish
February 20–March 20

Smelly

Truths Uttered by Savvy Humans, or We Couldn't Have Put It Better Ourselves

"Cats seem to go on the principle that it never does any harm to ask for what you want."

—Joseph Wood Krutch,
The Twelve Seasons, 1949

"Of all God's creatures there is only one that cannot be made the slave of the lash. That one is the cat. If man could be crossed with the cat it would improve man, but it would deteriorate the cat."

—Mark Twain,
Notebook, 1935

Chicken Soup

People rely so much on chicken soup to make them feel better. To cheer the spirit, cure the common cold, and warm the cockles of their giant hearts. As they are indulging themselves with a large bowl of hot chicken broth (with or without giblets), I watch them and wonder why they do not share some with me.

I love to eat chicken. My people generously serve me prekilled chicken from cans on a regular basis. Chicken is a large bird with a deadly beak and is very rare in the wild, so I have never caught one on my own. I can only imagine the effect of sucking down warm chicken juices on a cold winter day. My soul grazes on the thought of what chicken soup might do for a cat. We may never know, my friends. A cat may know everything and everyone there is to know, but chicken soup may forever remain beyond his reach. Do your best to try to get some while you're in this life. Put your paw on the spoon in the hands of your human. And when or if you succeed, please share your experience with the rest of us.

And if you do not ever taste chicken soup, take

heart, for we possess the pleasures of catnip, and the people do not.

I hope you have enjoyed these morsels of inspiration. And I hope you'll send me a kitty tale, perhaps one that helped you through an important time in your life.

Don't forget to feed your soul. Breathe deep the flowering catnip all around you.

Until we meet again.

— *Woody*

Hi Cats—

I know you're out there. Share your true stories with me. It would be an honor to share them with other cats. I love you.

—W.

Send cards and letters to:

Woody
c/o William Morrow
1350 Avenue of the Americas
New York, NY 10019

Woody is an orange-and-white cardigan sweater tomcat, born in 1985. He spent most of his life in New York City and is now spending his fourth life on a barrier island off South Carolina. Jane O'Boyle is one of Woody's people. She is a writer who lives near Charleston.